Five Little Ladybugs

By Pam Schiller and Richele Bartkowiak

Illustrated by Michelle Ciappa

Hi, I'm Noodlebug. Are you ready to "use your noodle?" Your "noodle" is your brain. You use it when you read or listen to stories.

Here's a special story about some friends of mine who love to dance and sing. I join them on one of the pages. See if you can find me!

School Specialty Publishing

Text © 2006 Noodlebug Productions LLC.
Art and Design © 2006° School Specialty Publishing.
Published by School Specialty Publishing, a member of the School Specialty Family.

Send all inquiries to School Specialty Publishing • 8720 Orion Place • Columbus, OH 43240-2111

ISBN 0-7696-4277-2

1 2 3 4 5 6 7 8 PHXBK 11 10 09 08 07 06

Five little ladybugs
dancing on the shore.
One danced away and
then there were four.

Four little ladybugs
dipping in the sea.
One chased a fish and
then there were three.

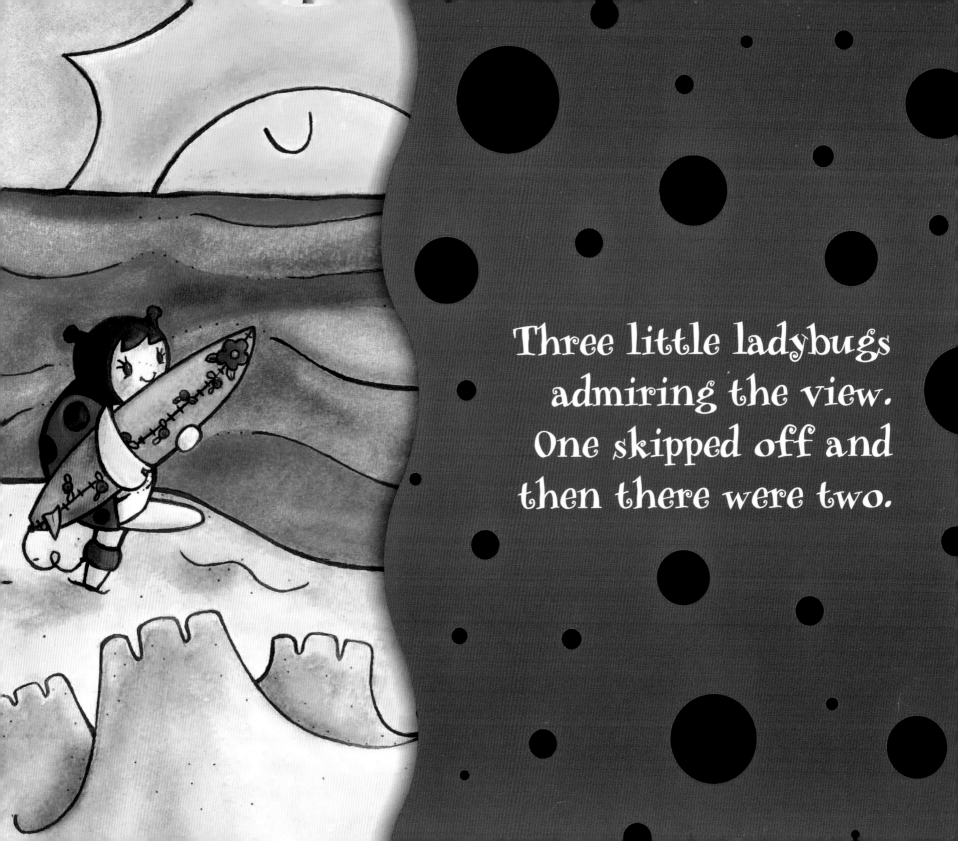

Three little ladybugs
admiring the view.
One skipped off and
then there were two.

Two little ladybugs
bathing in the sun.
One flew home,
leaving only one.

One little ladybug
all alone.
She called her friends
on the telephone.

They all came back
—one through five—

to dance and sing the
"Ladybug Jive!"

We had a great time doing the Ladybug Jive!
Next time, try singing the words to the tune
"Five Little Ducks." Singing is good for your brain,
and it helps make things easier to remember.
See you again soon, and don't forget to "use your noodle!"